CHARI
AND THE AMAZING PROFESSOR PLUM

CHAPTER 1

A TALL STORY

"Now that should do the trick," said Jeremy. "Yes, yes, I think that should do very nicely."

It was Jeremy's birthday and he was overjoyed to have been given the present that he'd always wanted. Secretly, he would have dispensed with the family get-together. But being the good-natured chap that he was, Jeremy had sat and smiled whilst everyone sang happy birthday. He'd blown out all the candles on his cake in one go. He hadn't tried to hide when his aunts queued to kiss his cheek. Nor was there any sign of a blush when Sarah, his little sister, read aloud all the good wishes on his birthday cards. And now that the fuss was finally over and after carefully opening a large cardboard box and removing its contents, Jeremy, at long last was the proud owner of a brand-new telescope.

"Yes, that should just about do it," fussed Jeremy, as he aimed the tube skyward and carefully adjusted the lens.

Now there must be thousands if not hundreds of thousands of telescopes all lovingly cherished by their owners, some probably costing a great deal of money.

This particular telescope however was very special. For this was no ordinary piece of tube with an optical lens. Not at all, this particular brand–new shiny telescope was Jeremy's and he loved it.

"Now let's see," said Jeremy. "It should be dark by about eight, and with Saturn in opposition, Orion will probably stand out like a sore thumb. Not only that!" shrieked Jeremy. "With a bit of luck --- there should be good visibility this evening."

"What's he rambling on about?" asked Sarah.

Charlie shrugged his shoulders, "something about writing a composition --- only he's got a sore thumb."

"Now then, one more final check and yes --- yes that should just about do nicely."

"May I look?" said Sarah.

"Well, there really isn't a lot to see right now but if you're very careful, I don't see why not."

Sarah closed one eye as she peered into the eyepiece of the brand–new shiny tube. "You're right Jeremy," said Sarah.

"What?" said Jeremy excitedly. "You agree --- we should see Saturn tonight!"

"No, you're right --- there's nothing much to see."

Jeremy folded his arms and sighed at his little sister.

"Can I have a turn?" said Charlie.

"Oh --- go ahead, but be very careful!" insisted Jeremy. "Sarah's right --- all you can see is sky ---."

"Well I know that," pleaded Jeremy, "but tonight ---."

"Wait a minute!" Charlie pulled his head sharply from the lens of Jeremy's telescope and rubbed his eyes." "I don't believe it!" said the little chimp.

"What did you see Charlie?" gasped Sarah.

Without answering Charlie put his eye close to the lens once more and peered out into the blue.

"No --- he's gone now --- I can't see him at all," said Charlie, as he twisted the long shiny tube in all directions.

"Careful!" snapped Jeremy.

"What do you mean --- you can't see him at all --- see who?" asked Sarah.

Charlie stared at his cousins.

"Oh no!" said Jeremy, "if this is another one of your stories."

Charlie clasped his hands behind his back and stared innocently at the ceiling.

"What did you see Charlie? --- Come on, tell!"

"Well ----," said Charlie. "I saw a man flying through the sky with a rocket on his back."

Jeremy and Sarah for a second or two stood silent then they fell to the floor with fits of laughter.

"Ha --- ha --- ha --- ha ---!" roared Jeremy.

"Charlie --- really," said Sarah.

"Oh dear --- you really can tell em," cried Jeremy.

"But I really did see a man with a rocket on his back," pleaded the little chimp. "Why don't you believe me?"

"Oh but we do! Don't we Sarah?" giggled Jeremy, winking to his little sister.

"Right!" said Charlie. "Don't believe me, see if I care!"

And the little chimp strode briskly for the door.

"Where are you going?" said Jeremy,

"I'm going home!" screeched the little chimp.

"Don't go Charlie it will spoil the party!" pleaded Sarah.

But it was too late. Charlie's feelings were hurt and he set off in a huff and slammed the door behind him.

"Now look what you've done!" screamed Sarah.

"What's going on you two?"

"It's Jeremy mum ---- he's upset Charlie."

"Oh really Jeremy – he's left without even taking a piece of birthday cake. How could you be so mean?"
"What?" said Jeremy.
"And to think, that he's your best friend too."
"But I -----."
"I'm going to play outside!" snapped Sarah.
And Jeremy was left alone with his beloved telescope.
"Really ----," muttered Jeremy. "A man flying through the sky with a rocket on his back. Who would believe such a whopper?"

"Why don't you believe me?" pleaded the little chimp.

4

CHAPTER 2

SEEING IS BELIEVING

Later that evening after all the guests had left it was finally time for Jeremy to explore the night sky.

This being a special occasion both he and Sarah had been given permission to stay up late. Jeremy almost shook with excitement at the prospect of actually seeing the planets that he'd read so much about.

"Pass me that book of star-charts please Sarah," said Jeremy.

"You mean the one that Charlie bought you for your birthday," scowled Sarah.

"Look, you laughed just as much as I did!" snapped Jeremy.

"Then we should both be ashamed of ourselves," said Sarah.

"But if he hadn't told such a whopper in the first place," protested Jeremy.

"What's Charlie been up to now?" inquired Jeremy's father, as he stretched and yawned.

"Well," giggled Jeremy, "he said he saw a man flying through the sky with a rocket on his back."

"Ha –ha –ha, that sounds like Charlie alright," said Jeremy's father. "Well, goodnight children. I'm going to bed. I hope you find that planet you've been rambling on about. What do they call it Sat--- Sat--something?"

"Saturn dad."

"Yes of course, goodnight children."

"Right," said Jeremy, rubbing his hands as though he was

about to embark on some great adventure.

"Now to explore the solar system."

Sarah forced a half-smile. After all, it was her brother's birthday and she so wanted him to enjoy his long awaited present.

"Just think Sarah," said Jeremy. "Once we can find our way around the night sky we'll be able to study Mars and Venus and Jupiter and ---."

"Yes but what about ---?" interrupted Sarah.

"and did you know that Jupiter has more moons than any other planet --- or is it ---?"

"Yes, but what about ---?"

"And did you know little sister that ---?"

"Yes! But what about Charlie?" screeched Sarah.

"Look," sighed Jeremy, "if it makes you feel any better we'll go over first thing in the morning and straighten things out, agreed?"

"Agreed," said Sarah.

"Right now let's get on," insisted Jeremy.

Feeling just a little more at ease Sarah sat back and watched patiently whilst her big brother explored the face of a beautiful waxing moon. She took great delight when Jeremy would suddenly jump up and dance around as his telescope found yet another lunar landmark that up to now he'd only read about.

"Look Sarah! --- Look!" he would cry.

And whilst Sarah took her turn to gaze at the barren craters Jeremy would hurriedly jot notes for future explorations.

Then with the help of his charts Jeremy would plot a course and the search would begin again. Sarah began to anticipate the sudden eruptions, as Jeremy's excited voice would start to tremble followed by fists punching the air. Then leaps and bounds that a ballet-dancer would have been proud of.

"I wonder what you'd look like in a tutu?" giggled Sarah.

"What?" said Jeremy.

"Oh never mind."

"Eureka," cried Jeremy. "Look Sarah I've found it!"

Sarah peered through the eyepiece of the bright shiny tube.

"Wow ---!" said Sarah.

Jeremy had certainly done his homework. For there in all its glory was the planet that Jeremy had dreamed of seeing with his very own eyes. There, in the lens of Jeremy's telescope was the ringed planet of Saturn.

"It's magnificent," admitted Sarah, in a trembling voice. Jeremy almost purred with satisfaction. He had scored a double victory. Not only had he found his dream planet but he had converted his little sister to enthusiast. No punching the air or leaping around now. Just quiet moments as brother and sister patiently took turns to track the planet that seemed to float like magic across the eyepiece of Jeremy's beloved telescope.

Hour after pleasant hour passed and only the occasional yawn briefly drowned the ticking of the clock as the small hours rolled on by.

"Come along Jeremy," said Sarah, "It really is time we went to bed."

"Oh, I suppose you're right," said Jeremy.

But as they reached the foot of the stair Jeremy stopped and smiled pleadingly at his little sister.

"I can't resist it," he whispered. "Just one last look before we go up."

Sarah helped herself to a slice of birthday cake as Jeremy tiptoed across the room. Jeremy rubbed his sleepy eyes then lowered his head for one last peek that would bring an end to a splendid evening, but suddenly the precious telescope came in for a bit of rough handling as Jeremy twisted it sharply.

"Jeremy! For goodness-sake what is it?" gasped Sarah.

Jeremy turned and stared blankly at his little sister. The smile he'd adopted since opening his birthday present had vanished. His face was gaunt and shocked.

"Jeremy, what did you see?"

Jeremy almost choked on a sharp gulp of breath.

"I --- I ---," stuttered Jeremy. "I saw a man --- flying through the sky with a rocket on his back!"

"I saw a man --- flying through the sky with rocket on his back!"

8

CHAPTER 3

MEET THE PROFESSOR

On a large swaying branch overhanging a gentle stream sat a forlorn little figure. Oblivious to his own sad reflection in the rippling water below, Charlie pondered the events of yesterday. 'How could Sarah and Jeremy have been so cruel? To laugh in his face and call him a liar.' It was all just a bit too much for the little chimp to bear.

"Who needs friends anyway?" cried Charlie, as he sprang to his feet and bounced violently on his makeshift perch. The little chimp had no-one to turn to with his woes. His closest friends had hurt him deeply and only the uncaring tree was to witness his pain, and as the little chimp lost control his head met with a knobbly branch. Stunned by the sudden thud Charlie tumbled through leafy branches and sank beneath the rippling water.

Fate however was to lend a hand and before the little chimp was lost to a watery grave a long spindly arm reached out and hauled him to safety.

"Have you got him Humble?"

"I have him professor!"

"Right now let me examine my patient. Yes --- just as I suspected, no real harm done."

Charlie, still dazed, coughed and spluttered.

"Don't be alarmed. You're safe now," said a squeaky child-like voice.

Charlie peered through waterlogged eyes to see who was the owner of that squeaky voice. There, knelt beside him was a strange looking figure. An elderly man dressed in white, apart from a pair of brown shoes that looked far too small to be related to their owner. A pair of piercing eyes that seemed to grow large and then small as they glared through thick black-rimmed spectacles. A large pink wrinkled head, bald, but above the ears a rim of thick spiky brown hair.
A moustache that could have easily been mistaken for a hedgehog with eyebrows to match. All this mounted on huge shoulders with no sign of a neck. Huge brown hairy hands protruded out of neatly creased sleeves. A gold watch with several dials stretched around a thick strong looking wrist.
"Permit me to introduce myself."
Charlie almost giggled as the huge man spoke. Surely that voice was an impostor. Charlie had vague memories of similar tones that accompanied a ventriloquist's dummy. However, the little chimp thought it best not to laugh. After all, this person whoever he was, had just saved his life.
"I am professor Plum and this is my assistant Humble."
"I am very pleased to make your acquaintance," said a tall gaunt figure, offering his hand to the little chimp.
"That will do Humble!" snapped the professor as he rose to his feet. It was then that Charlie got the greatest shock of all, for this huge man was not huge at all. In fact he was shorter by far than any grown up Charlie knew. A stunted Hercules.
"It was a good job for my sake that you were passing sir," said Charlie.
"You may address me, as professor, young man!"

Charlie was trying to be polite and thank his new acquaintances, but the overwhelming presence of this strange character made Charlie uneasy.

"To clarify matters, Humble and I, were not merely passing," squeaked the professor.

"Indeed, if it were not for my ---."

"Professor, someone's coming," said Humble, pointing a bony finger towards a thick cluster of trees.

"More interruptions!" snapped the professor.

"How does he know someone's coming?" asked Charlie. "I can't see anyone."

"As I was about to say before I was so rudely interrupted!" The professor stared menacingly at his colleague as a teacher would towards a pupil who had just misbehaved.

"If you will note young man my assistant has in his hands a very clever device. A little invention of mine," said the professor, puffing out his huge chest as if to invite applause.

"That device provides images by detecting heat just as it detected you as you fell into the stream --- wasting my valuable time, I may add."

"There are two of them professor."

"Yes alright Humble, don't mumble!" snapped the professor.

It seemed to Charlie that Humble's life was one of reprimand. No matter what he said or did a squeaky voice was quick to snap.

"Now if you will pay attention," said the professor, snatching the heat signalling device out of his assistants hand.

"You will observe that two heat sources are about to appear, just, about --- now!"

"Sarah! Jeremy!" cried Charlie, "over here."

"You are acquainted with these heat sources," squeaked the professor.

"Oh yes," said Charlie, "there're my best ----."

"Yes?" said the professor, as the little chimp cut short his sentence.

"Well you see," said Charlie, "they were my best friends, but---."

"Don't tell me," squeaked the professor. "You had an argument."

"Well, sort of," said Charlie.

"Hello Charlie," said Sarah, as she and Jeremy slowly approached.

"Hi Charlie," said Jeremy. "We were on our way over to apologise little cousin."

"We really are sorry," said Sarah.

"Oh forget it," said Charlie.

"Yes, but you see Charlie after you left, I saw him."

"May I ask whom, you saw?" inquired the professor, bowing to the new arrivals in a sarcastic sort of way.

"Sarah, Jeremy, this is---."

"I am professor Plum and this is my assistant Grumble."

"Humble, sir."

"What!" snapped the professor?

"Forgive me sir, I thought you said Grumble."

"I've told you before Humble, don't mumble!"

"Yes sir, very sorry sir," sighed Humble.

The chimps put their hands to their mouths.

"Now young man if you would kindly tell me who you saw and then if there are no more interruptions," said the professor, staring at his hapless assistant, "then I can get on with the work that I came here to do in the first place."

"Well," said Jeremy. "Last night I saw a man flying through the sky ---."

"Yes, yes, go on," snapped the professor.

"Well you probably won't believe me sir," said Jeremy. "But I saw someone flying in space with a sort rocket on his back."

"And how may I ask did you manage to see such a small object at such a distance?" squeaked the professor.

"With my telescope sir," replied Jeremy. "The one I got yesterday for my birthday."

The professor smiled warmly at Jeremy. Until now he had acted like a frustrated headmaster who was sick of children, but when this man smiled it was like a ray of sunshine.

"You did not see just anyone flying through the sky last night," squeaked the professor. "What you saw was my latest invention. I call it, The Backpack Space Explorer."

"Wow!" said the chimps. "That was you?"

The professor puffed out his huge chest as he sensed admiration.

"Humble, please be so kind as to collect the silver metallic box from our stores. Gather round," said the professor. "I have something very special show you."

The obedient Humble soon returned and handed over a box no bigger than a small suitcase. The professor beckoned the chimps towards him as he placed the box carefully on the ground.

"Now, watch closely," whispered the professor, as he flipped open a pair of clips. Suddenly the box burst open.
In seconds a large table with six chairs unfolded. Cakes, buns, drinks and all sorts of good things just seemed to appear out of nowhere.
"There, ready for any emergency," squeaked the professor. "Happy birthday! Come along Humble, join the party!"
The chimps doubted whether the professor was a serious inventor or someone who had dropped out of the circus. However one thing was for sure the buns and cakes were delicious.
"Wow!" said Sarah. "How did all this lot come out of that little box?"
"Who cares," said Charlie, as he helped himself to lemonade.
"Thank you professor," said Jeremy, "This is amazing!"

Suddenly the box burst open

CHAPTER 4

THE MAN WHO WAS AFRAID OF --- ?

"Oh my," said Sarah, as she tucked away the last piece of cream cake. "That was delicious."

"It certainly was," said Jeremy.

Charlie and Humble nodded in agreement.

"Well if everyone's finished?" squeaked the professor, staring around the table. "Time to get on. Stand back everyone!"

The professor flipped open the lid of the silver box and within seconds the table chairs cups plates spoons, all disappeared back into place as the lid snapped shut.

"Humble, you may return this to our stores."

But as the professor bent down to pick up the box he stopped as if frozen on the spot.

"What's wrong professor?" asked Charlie.

"Humble, Humble," squeaked the professor through closed lips.

"What is it, what's wrong?" asked Sarah.

"Professor are you alright?" said Jeremy.

"Humble, what's wrong with the professor?" cried Charlie.

Humble sauntered across to his employer with deliberate ease.

"Is this what's bothering you sir?" said Humble, as he picked a tiny spider off the silver box.

"Remove it at once!" squeaked the professor.
Humble smirked at the chimps as he carried off the tiny wriggling creature. The professor blinked through his thick spectacles at his little audience.
"I'm afraid it's true," admitted the professor.
"True sir?" said Sarah.
"Arachnophobia," squeaked the professor.
"What?" said Charlie.
"He's afraid of spiders," said Jeremy.
"Terrified of them," sighed the professor.
The chimps stared at each other in silence. It was hard to believe that this incredible man could be afraid of anything, but to tremble at a harmless little spider.
"Well, let's get on," squeaked the professor, as he wiped his brow with a large handkerchief, "I have something very important to show you."
Charlie had visions of more good things to eat appearing out of nowhere. The professor's face however now looked serious. Humble reappeared after his eviction duties and along with the chimps followed the professor to a small clearing.
Hidden beneath a large camouflaged net stood three black boxes.
"Now whatever you do," insisted the professor, "make sure you don't trip or tug the rope or the net will drop instantly and tangle everything."
Sarah took Charlie by the hand.
"What you see is the result of several years hard work," said the professor, as he unclipped the first box and began

assembling an assortment of tubes. The chimps watched excitedly. Soon it was obvious that these three small boxes housed the machine that Charlie and Jeremy had seen flying through the night sky.

"You see," said the professor, "my invention eliminates the need for large crews that are normally required for space exploration. It eliminates the huge amount of fuel that costs a fortune. In fact my method is so simple it's sheer-genius!"

 It occurred to the chimps that although this man had a lot of qualities, modesty was definitely not one of them.

"Tonight I shall make the final test before showing the world my revolutionary design."

"Thank goodness," muttered Humble to himself.

"Did I hear a grumble Humble?" snapped the professor.

"Of course not sir."

"Then go and collect my notes, and Humble."

"Yes sir,"

"Don't fumble!"

"Yes sir, I mean no sir."

Charlie and Jeremy couldn't help but giggle, but Sarah saw things a little different.

"Must you be so hard on him?"

"There-there Clara no need to get upset," said the professor.

"It's Sarah if you don't mind, and I am upset!"

"Well, if it will make amends my dear, the very moment he returns I'll tell him I'm sorry."

That moment was quicker by far than the professor could have anticipated. For suddenly the tall figure of Humble burst through the little group, his legs carrying him as fast as they could go.

"Run professor! Run everyone!"

"Humble!" screeched the professor. "Where are my notes? Come back at once! Humble you're fired! Do you hear me Humble? You're dismissed!"

"Something's really frightened him," said Sarah.

That something, suddenly, made its appearance.

With a terrifying roar a huge lion thundered into the little clearing, its back arched ready to pounce. In its eyes the reflection of a plump figure clad in white.

"Look out professor!" screamed the chimps.

But the man who was afraid of spiders simply smiled as he reached into his jacket pocket. As the lion pounced, a bright light and a strange buzzing sound filled the air.

"Ready for any eventuality," said the professor.

The chimps, huddled together, had instinctively backed away. They couldn't believe what they had just seen. In the professor's right hand was something that looked like a gun. In his left hand was a very tiny lion.

"Just one of my little inventions," said the professor. "I call it my molecule accelerating activator."

"You mean that thing turned the lion into a kitten?" asked Sarah.

"Not exactly Clara, I mean Sarah. If you look closely you will see that he's exactly the same only smaller.

The little lion wriggled in the grasp of a brown hairy hand.

"That's amazing!" said Charlie.

"But what about the lion?" asked Jeremy. "Will he return to his normal size?"

A hairy sausage of a finger beckoned the chimps to follow. The professor placed the tiny cat on the ground and along with the chimps retreated to a safe distance.

"Now all I have do is press the reverse button on my Molecule Accelerating Activator aim, and --- wait a minute --- would you like to do the honours?" said the professor, smiling at Charlie.

"Yes please!" said the little chimp.

"Just point it like a gun and press the trigger once."

Charlie did just that and with a flash of bright light accompanied by loud buzzing, the lion, was restored to his normal size. The big cat a little dazed shook his head then went on his way no worse for his experience.

"Right!" said the professor, smiling at the chimps. "Back to work."

As the lion pounced a bright light and a strange buzzing noise filled the air

CHAPTER 5

NOTHING TO FEAR

"Humble!" called the professor. "You can come out now there's nothing to be afraid of."

"Come out come out wherever you are," cried Charlie.

The little group had returned to the clearing but there was no sign of the professor's faithful servant.

"Humble!" cried the professor once more. You may return to your duties. There's nothing to f---f ---fear."

The chimps stared as the professor froze on the spot.

"What is it professor, what's wrong?" said Jeremy.

"Look!" said Sarah.

The chimps gasped. Clambering its way over a black box directly in front of the professor was the thing he feared the most.

"It's a tarantula!" screamed Jeremy.

"Back away professor!" cried Sarah.

But the professor was stricken with fear and unable to move. He knew that one bite from this hairy predator and it would be curtains. His brilliant brain pleaded to his limbs to move, but his body was unable to obey.

"Quick do something," screamed Sarah.

Jeremy looked around for a stick or something to throw.

"The molecule whatever it is!" screamed Sarah. "The gun!"

"Use it Charlie," cried Jeremy. "Reduce it to the size of a flea and I'll stand on it."

"Hurry!" screamed Sarah.

Charlie pointed the gun and fired. Unfortunately the little chimp in his haste had forgotten the professor had pressed the reverse button and the killer spider grew instantly to the size of a lion.

"Oh no!" screamed Sarah.

"Now what?" cried Charlie.

"Press a button!" screamed Sarah. "Press a button and fire again. Quickly!"

Charlie stabbed at the buttons and fired at the oversize spider. To the horror of everyone the spider now grew to the size of an elephant.

"You must have pressed the wrong button!" said Jeremy.

"Here, let me look," screamed Sarah, as she snatched the gun from her cousin's shaky hand.

"Look, it's there, Normal, Reverse!" cried Sarah, and she fired as fast as she could. Sarah had kept a cool head and hit the right button. Unfortunately she hit the wrong target and the professor shrank to the size of a mouse.

Sarah, shocked by what she'd done, stumbled backwards and the gun went flying from her tiny hand.

"What now?" screamed Charlie.

The monster spider was about to strike. The professor, stricken with fear, was unable to move.

The monster spider was about to strike

CHAPTER 6

A HUMBLING EXPERIENCE

Jeremy knew that he'd only a split second in which to save the professor. Somehow this brilliant man had to be rescued. But how, what was to be done? Everything so far had failed. Charlie had turned the killer spider into a monster. Sarah had turned the professor into a manikin and there was no sign of Humble. All these thoughts bounced around within Jeremy's head, when suddenly he remembered the professor's warning. 'Whatever you do, don't trip or tug the rope, or the net will drop instantly.'

"That's it!" screamed Jeremy, and he hurled himself at the rope and gave it a mighty tug.

The huge net dropped just as the professor said it would and the mighty spider became its prisoner. It wriggled and twisted franticly to make its escape but the more it wriggled the more entangled it became. Jeremy as gently as he could gathered the professor in cupped hands and the chimps backed away as the spider wrestled in vain.

"Now it knows what it feels like to be in a web!" said Jeremy.

"Are you alright professor?" said Sarah.

"My Molecule Accelerator!" pleaded a tiny squeaky voice. "Return me to my normal size, quickly!"

"Allow me sir."

"Humble!" cried the chimps. "Are we glad to see you?"

The professor's faithful servant had at last returned.

"First things first," said Humble.

Two flashes of bright light accompanied by loud buzzing saw the killer spider restored to its normal size. The hairy predator now able to slip through the camouflage net beat a hasty retreat.

"Now me Humble!" squeaked the professor.

Jeremy, very carefully placed the professor on the ground and the chimps stood clear.

"Get on with it Humble!" snapped the professor.

"Yes sir, of course sir, immediately, if not sooner," said Humble, as he slowly walked a circle around his tiny employer.

"Well, what are you waiting for?"

"Well, now that you come to mention it sir, there are one-or-two things I would like to bring to your attention."

"Don't mumble Humble," ranted the professor, return me to my normal size immediately or, or---."

"Or, what?" said Humble, twirling the gun around his finger as though he was a wild west hero.

The professor gave a very tiny gulp.

"Perhaps sir," said Humble. "If you were to show a little politeness on occasion. Perhaps even a little appreciation."

"But Humble, I've always had the highest regard for your services." pleaded the professor.

"Have you indeed?" said Humble.

"Yes of course I have old chap."

"Then what about my salary?"

"What about your salary?" squeaked the professor.

"Well to start with I'd like one!"

The professor's tiny face turned crimson as three little pairs of dark round eyes stared.

"Really professor," said Sarah.

"Return me to my normal size immediately and we'll discuss it," squeaked the professor, folding his tiny arms and stamping the ground.

"I think not," said Humble.

The professor beckoned his assistant towards him.

Humble leant an ear obligingly and the professor whispered into it.

"Try again professor," snapped Humble.

"Really Humble," squeaked the professor.

"Try again!" demanded Humble.

The professor whispered once more into the giant ear.

"That will do admirably sir," said Humble. "Stand back everyone."

And before you could say 'Giant Spider' the professor was his normal self once more.

"Thank you Humble old chap."

"It's this little fellow you should be thanking," said Humble, patting Jeremy on the back.

"Yes, if it wasn't for you young man, I would have been dessert for that great hairy beast. How can I ever repay you?" said the professor, smiling at Jeremy.

"No thanks necessary professor."

"Indeed there is young Jeremy. Now that Humble is content and may I add grossly overpaid," snapped the professor, "it's time for your reward."

"Tell me, what was it exactly you were observing with that telescope of yours?"

"He's absolutely over the moon about Saturn," said Sarah.

"Is that a fact young Jeremy?" asked the professor.

"It is indeed sir. I've longed to see Saturn and ---."

"That will do young man. Humble, go and collect the two red-boxes from our stores and Humble! Don't ---!"

Humble stared blankly at his employer.

"I --- I mean Humble old chap. Would you please be so kind as to collect the two red boxes from our stores?"

Humble smiled at the chimps. "With pleasure sir."

It wasn't long before the now grossly overpaid Humble returned with two suitcase-sized boxes.

"Here you are young Jeremy, try this for size," said the professor, as he handed Jeremy what looked like a suit made of tinfoil. "There, fits like a glove."

"But what's this all about sir," asked Jeremy.

"You said you wanted to see Saturn and so you shall," said the professor. "With just these few accessories my back-pack unit grows large enough to carry two. I call it the ---!"

"Yes?" said the chimps.

"Well, I'm not quite sure what to call it yet, but I'll think of something."

Humble helped the professor as pipes and tubes hissed loudly as they locked into position.

"Just our helmets and then we're ready. Can you hear me? Testing one two three."

"Loud and clear professor!" said Jeremy.

"Then we're ready!"

"Stand back everyone!" shouted Humble.

Sarah and Charlie covered their ears as the ground started to tremble. Then like a bullet from a gun Jeremy and the professor were shot into space.

"Will they be OK?" asked Sarah.

"Of course they will my dear," said Humble. "The professor has full control. All your little friend has to do is enjoy the ride."

At that particular moment Jeremy was anything but enjoying the ride. He felt as though he was being crushed as the sudden pressure of being launched into space suddenly hit him. Then, after a little dizziness he shook his head and peered through the window of his helmet. He gasped, as he saw the

"Wow!" cried Jeremy. "There she is! Rings and all!"

27

earth shrinking below him. Then the moon suddenly grew large and then small again as the professor's rocket blasted them at terrific speed into the heavens.

"Close your eyes and keep them closed," said the professor. Jeremy's whole body trembled with excitement.

"You may look now!"

"Wow!" cried Jeremy. "There she is! Rings and all!"

It was a dream come true. Jeremy gazed in awe at the magnificent sight that the professor had gifted him.

"Thank you professor! Thank you!" cried Jeremy.

"Oh it's nothing," said the professor.

"Nothing! It's out of this world," said Jeremy.

"If you say so," said the professor, in his squeaky little voice, "but you must keep this little trip our secret."

"It's a promise," said Jeremy.

"Look they're back!" said Humble, pointing a long bony finger skywards. " Stand clear everyone!"

Sarah and Charlie breathed a sigh of relief as Jeremy and the professor touched down gently and safely.

Jeremy couldn't wait to get out of his suit and share his adventure with everyone.

"You do realise professor we'll never hear the end of this," said Sarah.

The professor and Humble shared a smile. Then a look of sadness overcame the great man's face.

"What is it professor?" asked Sarah.

Instead of answering, the professor each in turn gave the little chimps a huge hug.

"I'm afraid it's time to say goodbye," said the professor.

Humble blushed as he saw a tear roll down his employer's chubby face.

"My work here is complete. I must now return home and write my notes. It would be selfish of me not to share my genius invention with the rest of mankind."

"Modest to the end." whispered Humble.

"Did you mumble Humble?" snapped the professor. "I --- I mean, did you say something old chap?"

Humble just smiled.

"We'll help you pack," said Sarah.

"No need Clara! I --- I mean Sarah, Humble and I can manage."

"Trot along and bring the jeep would you old chap?" said the professor. "I'll sort things here."

With a few clicks on what looked like a TV remote, boxes just seemed to pack themselves. Lids folded with absolute precision and slammed shut.

"There, how's that?" said the professor.

"Ready for any eventuality!" said the chimps in one voice.

Humble arrived in the jeep and began loading for the journey home.

"You will be kind to him won't you professor?" said Sarah.

"Of course I will my dear."

Charlie and Jeremy smiled.

"We're all packed and ready to go professor," said Humble.

"Then this really is goodbye. Now take good care of yourselves," said the professor.

"Goodbye, we'll miss you," said Humble.

"Come along Humble!" said the professor, "and Humble."

"Yes sir."

"Don't stumble!"

"Yes sir. I mean no sir."

Charlie, Sarah and Jeremy waved goodbye until the jeep was completely out of sight.

"Well, I guess it's time we made tracks," said Charlie.

Sarah and Jeremy nodded in agreement and the trio set off for home.

"Night Charlie, sleep well," said Sarah.

"Night little cousin," said Jeremy. "Why don't you sleep over tomorrow-night?"

"And play with the telescope?" said Charlie.

"Absolutely!"

"Great!" said Charlie, "See you tomorrow."

That night Jeremy stared into a blank dismal sky.

"Nothing to see tonight little fellow," said Jeremy's father.

Jeremy smiled in reply as he dusted the long shiny tube that sat beside him.

"By the way son, did you mange to see Saturn?"

"Oh yes indeed father!" Jeremy almost screamed. "I can honestly say that I've seen Saturn like no-one else!"

Jeremy desperately wanted to tell of his exploits but he'd made a promise, a promise that had to be kept.

"Well it's bedtime son. Sarah's fast asleep already."

"Coming right up dad."

Jeremy took one last look into the empty sky. Would he ever again see anyone flying in space with a rocket strapped to their back?

Would the long suffering Humble ever get his salary?

Would the professor share his invention with the world or would he fly off to some strange world by himself? If he did, Jeremy hoped for his sake that wherever he landed, there would be no spiders. A huge smile found its way onto Jeremy's face as he made his way upstairs. At least there was one thing he was absolutely sure about. There was no doubt whatsoever that the time spent with professor Plum was truly amazing.

THE END
Other titles to add to your collection.

And for the younger reader:

Watch out for Charlie's next adventure!:

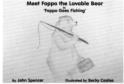

Charlie
and the Dream-pool

Illustrations digitally remastered and coloured by Ben Reed.

Printed by, Hackett & Williamson
94-96 Alezadra Road, Hull
England

The 'Charlie the Chimp' Series is published by: **FLINTON PRESS.**
17 Ullswater Drive, Gillshill Road, Kingston Upon Hull HU8 0JZ. (England)

To view more of our children's books, and browse the rest of the Charlie Collection, Find us online, at Flinton Press